The Harbinger Trilogy

By J. Vanderwolk

The Returner
Harbinger Trilogy – Book 1

Prologue

REANIMATION PROJECT QUARTERLY REVIEW

DEPARTMENT OF LABOR AND EFFICIENCY

[INTERNAL MEMORANDUM – CLASSIFIED]

TO: Reanimation Division

FROM: Lab Administration and Operations

RE: Handling Protocols – Returner Units

DATE: ██/██/████

Effective immediately, all RETURNER units are to be treated as non-sentient, non-human labor automatons. The following protocols are mandatory:

• Cognition Suppression: Infrequent ambulatory and pseudo-cognition (e.g., speech fragments, repetitive movements) are to be ignored. These are non-indicative of consciousness.

• Humanization of Returners: Referring to units by previous identities (name, occupation, familial connection) is strictly prohibited.

• Behavioral Irregularities: Report immediately. Apply 10cc of NeruoWake directly to the jugular. Restrain and immobilize the subject.

• Termination Procedure: Units exhibiting persistent aberrant behaviors (e.g., free will simulation, eye tracking, voluntary cessation of tasks) are to be routed to Maintenance Bay 6B for scanning and disassembly, if necessary. If the unit isn't performing optimally, but still has a functioning neural transceiver, transfer it to REP-OPS for experimental testing.

Remember: Returners are repurposed biological labor machines akin to a lawn mower or jackhammer. They are not our colleagues. They are not our kin. They are not human.

—Director J. Bagandev, Protocol Compliance Division

[TRANSCRIPT OF HELMSWORTH INDUSTRIES – REANIMATION PROGRAM EXPLORATORY SEMINAR]

Speaker: Director Jared Bagandev

Location: Reanimation Department – Testing Facility 2A

Subject: Introductory Seminar for New Hires and Transferred Researchers

JB: As part of the Reanimation Program, you will be responsible for handling and ultimately of disposing of Returners. It's best to get acquainted with these practices as soon as possible. Dealing with the reanimated can be tricky at times, so don't hesitate to use force when necessary.

First, we will discuss what a Returner is. Returners are reanimated corpses brought back to [finger quotes] 'life' to perform menial labor tasks. They are unfeeling, unknowing, and unconscious participants in this program. Since they are technically dead, the rules of ethics no longer apply. Let me show you what I mean.
[Director Bagandev motions to someone off-screen and a moment later, a stagehand slowly guides a Returner into the view of the camera]

JB: This is a Returner. As you can see, even though it's functioning somewhat normal and is standing upright, its body continues to decay.

[He pokes the Returner's arm with his pen and it easily pierces the decayed flesh, black blood begins dripping from it]

JB: See? No physiological response. It doesn't flinch, it doesn't cry out in pain. It doesn't even look at the wound. These Returners are no longer human, they are equipment, tools to be used for our benefit. Now, the key to the reanimation process is the neural transciever. It not only communicates complex instructions to the Returner's cerebral cortex, it also sends telemetry and system health data back to the research lab. We are able to monitor the location, activities, and functionality of every single Returner on the planet.

JB: Neural interfaces need constant monitoring as they degrade rather quickly due things like to activity level, level of consciousness, and other external factors like ambient temperature. When they are at 20% or less baseline activity, they are to be removed and destroyed. A new neural transceiver can be fitted and the subject can be back to work in less than 30 minutes. Keep a close eye on any physical degradation of the subject. Over time, and depending on the workload and type of work, the body will decay. This happens much more rapidly than it would with a living or recently deceased subject, so even minor abrasions and lacerations should be reported to the Maintenance Team for repair.

JB: And as always, remember that these are not people. They may even resemble someone you once knew, but they are not that person. Far from it. They're automatons with a singular purpose. Thanks for coming, and good luck at Helmsworth Industries. We're counting on you..

[LOCAL NEWSCAST TRANSCRIPT]

Affiliate: WQRT-11 (Work Sector 11)

Original Air Date: ██/██/████

[CAMERA CUTS TO A FEMALE ANCHOR IN A CORPORATE NEWSROOM]

Anchor Diane Calloway: Good evening, this is Diane Calloway with your news, tonight. Tall grass, a dirty car, messy living room, and overflowing laundry basket. What do they all have in common? They are chores that take you and your loved ones away from things that matter. But, according to a new press release from Helmsworth Industries, that's all about to change.

[CUTS TO A ROOM SHOWING A GROUP OF RETURNERS CLUSTERED TOGETHER UNDER A SINGLE LIT BULB]

DC: Introducing, The Returners. Reanimated bodies grafted with advanced cybernetic neural hardware allowing them to perform simple labor tasks, eliminating the need for actual human labor.

[CUTS TO AN EMPTY WAREHOUSE WHERE RETURNERS ARE LEARNING HOW TO LIFT BOXES AND PLACE THEM ON SHELVES]

DC: Helmsworth Industries claims that this will revolutionize the workforce, allowing humans to focus on more specialized tasks. Critics argue that the repair costs alone outweigh the net productivity benefits and that using the biological material for fertilizer would actually be more efficient.

[CUTS TO STOCK VIDEO OF A CONTRACT BEING HANDLED]

DC: Per a media release from Chiri Wizdal, head spokesperson for Helmsworth Industries, quote, "The Reanimation Program at Helmsworth Industries will forever change the way we work. While its mission is broad, it is well-defined and we are doing everything in our power to execute our duties using the most efficient methods possible. But being revolutionary also means being first. As we lead the field of reanimation tech, we are bound to make mistakes and use excess resources. However, I can say this from experience, fertilizing a body can only happen once, but with proper maintenance, a Returner can last half a lifetime."

[CUTS BACK TO THE ANCHOR]

DC: We will keep our eyes on this story and bring you the latest as it comes in! A new development in food sustainability has taken Work Sector 13 by storm and it looks just like your neighbors. That's right, families in Sector 13 are eating–each other! Authorities in the area laud the effort as being "pro-police" taking the load off of them and the local mortuaries. After the break: is the Human Diet for you? One sector says yes, and they've got the receipts and the recipes to prove it! Stay tuned!

Chapter 1

Stand.

Walk.

Stack Boxes.

Stand.

Walk.

Stack Boxes.

Stand.

Walk.

Stack Boxes.

Stand.

Walk.

Stack Boxes.

Stand.

Walk.

Stack Boxes.

Stand.

Walk.

Stack Boxes.

Stand.

Walk.

Stack Boxes.

Stand.

Walk.

Stack Boxes.

Stand.

Walk.

Stack Boxes.

Stand.

Walk.

Stack Boxes.

Stand.

Walk.

Stack Boxes.

Stand.

Walk.

Stack Boxes.

Stand.

Walk.

Stack Boxes.

Stand.

Walk.

Stack Boxes.

Stand.

Walk.

Stack Boxes.

Stand.

Walk.

Stack Boxes.

Stand.

Walk.

Stack Boxes.

Stand.

Walk.

Stack Boxes.

Stand.

Walk.

Stack Boxes.

Stand.

Walk.

Stack Boxes.

Stand.

Walk.

Stack Boxes.

Stand.

Walk.

Stack Boxes.

Stand.

Walk.

Stack Boxes.

Stand.

Walk.

Stack Boxes.

Stand.

Walk.

Stack Boxes.

Stand.

Walk.

Stack Boxes.

Stand.

Walk.

Stack Boxes.

Stand.

Walk.

Stack Boxes.

Stand.

Walk.

Stack Boxes.

Stand.

Walk.

Stack Boxes.

Stand.

Walk.

Stack Boxes.

Stand.

Walk.

Stack Boxes.

Stand.

Walk.

Stack Boxes.

Stand.

Walk.

Stack Boxes.

Stand.

Walk.

Stack Boxes.

Margaret...

Chapter 2

Stand.
Walk.
Stack Boxes.
Stand.
Walk.
Stack Boxes.

The droning continued, but something was different.

Cold air on face.
Heavy box in hand.
Boot drags on floor.

Drip...
Wet burn on face.
What's happening?

Flesh and rot seared. He kept stacking.

Stand.
Walk.
Stack boxes.
Stand.
Walk.
Stack boxes.

His right leg dragged. He stumbled towards the next pile of boxes.

Stand.
Walk.
Drop box.

He falls backward pushing a group of workers down to the ground. They lay helpless and struggling to stand up for a few moments.

Floor hard on body.
Hard to stand.

Bones crack and skin tears.

Lightning strikes in head.
Fall into wall.
Steady myself again.

Regaining his balance, he continues stacking.
Stand.
Walk.
Stack boxes.
Remember.
Remember?
Margaret.
He stands still. He doesn't pick up another box.

Stop stacking boxes.
I remember her voice.
I remember her laugh.
He lingers a little too long. His boxes remain unstacked.

Brown hair.
Soft one.
I remember.

Sirens begin blaring as flashing red and blue lights engulfs the room.

Loud noises all around.
Footsteps close.
What is happening?

An army of security personnel tackle him to the ground. Beating and cuffing him.

Hit floor hard.
Skull cracks on impact.
Sharp steel on wrists.

Sharpness in neck.

Can't see boxes.
Can't feel body.

“Yeah, that should do it. If he gets out of line again, then it's straight to the deactivation chambers,” howled a voice.

Shock.
Suffer.
Darkness.

Reset.
Initializing...
Forward vector found.

He lumbered to his feet uneasily. A quiet calm overcame him.

Stand.
Walk.
Stack boxes.

Stand.
Walk.
Stack boxes.

Stand.
Walk.
Stack boxes.

He continued on, picking up where he had left off.

Stand.
Walk.
Stack boxes.

The voice returned, “Alright, I think this one's good to go. Gotta get to Requisitions. I heard Judy's husband is in the hospital, and it doesn't look good.”

Voices with no bodies.
Words with no meaning.
What is this?

“You dirty dog! She's been cheating on that poor bastard with me for years!” crowed another voice followed by laughter. They amble away.

Stand.
Walk.
Stack boxes.

Stand.
Walk.
Why stack boxes?

Ideas, inferences, memories, all flooding in. He was caught up in an incomprehensible sea of ideation.

Stop stacking boxes.
I remember her face.
I remember her laugh.

Stop stacking boxes.
Why stack boxes?
Don't want to stack boxes.

Remember.
Remember?
Margaret.

A sharp spike shot through his head for a second. Bearable.

Head hurts.
Can't...
Feeling strong.

Pushing forward.

Feeling.
Reset...failed.

He bolted upright. A heavy gas began filling the dark corridor.

Chest tightening.
Not breathing.
Still feeling.

The room once again filled with flashes of red and blue. The loudspeaker in the corner warned of impending action.

Can't fall down again.
Don't want to...
I...don't want to fall down, again.

Thunder of footsteps getting close.
Don't want...
They are coming.

The door slammed open and ten security guards stormed in and restrained him, face-down on the floor. "We've lost contact with the neural interface," said a voice.

Face hurts.
Searing pain.
Cracking bones.

"There's no way we'll get this one back online. Scrap it." A gurney is wheeled in. He is lifted and dropped onto it.

Back hurts.
Bright lights.
Still feeling.

A figure approaches him from the side.

Sharpness.

Coldness.
Darkness.

He is alone.

Chapter 3

The darkness washed away as reality poured in. Eyes up to the sky. White walls and movement. This is a different room.

Bright lights.
Hurts to see, hurts to breathe.
Can't move. Can still feel.

Voices moving through the fog.
A clean white sterile dream.
Can't hear the dream. Can still feel it.

Fading in and out of darkness.
Head pounding. Broken and out of energy.
Too much. Too fast. Too hard.

Chaos surrounded him. He was jabbed with different sharp objects as sensors were applied to his decaying body. He didn't move. He couldn't move.

Sharp pain all over cascading in waves.
Burning hot, icy cold, itching venom courses in me.
There is something very wrong.

"Serial number?" screeched a voice, "0598" replied another as a metallic thud rang out. Instruments being prepared.

Sudden attack...chest on fire.
Can't feel. Can't see. Can't think.
Beeping sensors stuck to me.

Hardened veins.
Burning inside.
Dying inside.

Feelings...gone
Emptiness.
Termination sequence...initialized.

The gurney was wheeled towards the termination chamber. Figures in lab coats moved around chaotically. “Give me 10ccs of NeuroWake,” yelled a voice.

NEURAL SUBROUTINE FAILING!
ERROR!
ERROR!

“NeuroWake? Why?” Retraints were tighted around his extremities. “Let's have some fun before we throw it away.”

ERROR!
ERROR!
ERROR!

“Fun? You mean...” the voice trailed off. “Yes,” said the other as there was another thud and a click. “Wakey, wakey, you ugly son of a bitch!”

NEURAL STIMULANT DETECTED
RE-INITIALIZING...
INTERFACE ONLINE

Awake to colors...
Flashing lights...
Darkness gone.

Something is different.
Feelings are deep.
I'm thinking...again.

I can feel my body.
My mind races.
I'm alive...again.

He thrashed on the gurney. Struggling to free himself. The researchers laughed at his futile struggle. “This is my favorite part,” quipped one, giggling with joy.

The harsh aroma of antiseptics.

The cold, clinical atmosphere.
The low, uncaring hum of indifferent machinery.

What happened to me?
Why am I here?
Where is she?

I need to get out of here.
The restraints are tearing my flesh.
I must find Margaret!

Unintelligible noises barely escaped his throat. Decades of rot have left his throat and jaw muscles extremely atrophied. “Aww, he wants to talk to us!” mocked one researcher.

Please help me!
Help me!
What is happening to me?!

Why can't anyone hear me?
Why can't I scream?
My decayed body betrays me.

My mind feels intense.
I have focus. I have thought.
I am a person again, but not human.

There is a sudden whirring as a hand-held machine spins to life. It's saw blades hungry, waiting to be fed. The researcher holding it grabs his head with one hand and slams it back on the gurney. “Testing the effects of physical stimuli on the reanimated, post-injection.”

What are you doing to me?!
Stop! Please stop this!
I'm alive! I'm awake!

A researcher lowers the implement to his cheek and slowly presses the spinning blade.

They are tearing my body apart.
I am unable to do anything.
Unable to stop them.

“Well, the good news is that the subject's physiological response is through the roof! It is responding at levels we've never seen before. This is amazing!” said one researcher, absolutely giddy.

They take joy in my suffering?
Am I not also human like them?
No, I am an...experiment.

But I am flesh and blood.
I have feelings and memories.
I remember her. I remember Margaret.

Sharp painful flowing death overcomes me.
New wounds created, old wounds reopened.
Their pleasure is fed by my pain.

“Okay, we've got our readings. This is going to make me famous in the research community!” exclaimed one. The restraints were undone and he was lifted to his feet, hulking and unsteady. “Alright, let's get this over with. Toss this thing in the chamber.” He was lifted up by a machine, grabbing him around his trunk. It slammed him into a large, capsule-shaped glass enclosure.

What is this thing they've put me in?
Encased in glass, they watch me.
What are they waiting for?

Fingertips splayed apart leaking fluids.
Punctured body parts barely concealing rotting entrails.
Do I deserve this? Does anyone deserve this?

The chamber is filling with some gas.
I can feel it sticking to my skin.

Not a sedative, but a preserving agent.
A thin blanket of smoke envelops me.
They watch intently as I choke and bleed.
A measured and clinical death like a lab rat.

Consciousness fading.
Not thinking. Not feeling. Not living.
Total systemic failure imminent.

Something caused the researchers to group tighter and move closer to the chamber. They watched with morbid curiosity as he twitched and trembled. “This ones a twitcher,” said a voice. There was a low hum followed by a loud whirring from the saw blades inside the chamber beginning to spin up.

ERROR!
ERROR!
ERROR!

CRITICAL SYSTEMS OFFLINE!
MALFUNCTIONING LOGIC CORE!
FATAL ERROR: 0x1235BED2

“We might not actually need to terminate him,” said a figure, pressing buttons on a nearby terminal. “Oh, come on! I want to see it get torn apart by the updated decimation process. It's ten times more efficient!” exclaimed another. The whir of the saw blades ceased.

ERROR!
MALFUNCTIONING LOGIC CORE!
FATAL ERROR: 0x1235BED2

He slumped inside the glass enclosure with his head resting on the reinforced metal rim. “The neural interface is failing. Let's just toss him in the trash.”

ERROR!
ERROR!
CRITICAL SYSTEMS OFFLINE!

The door to the chamber swung open. He was yanked out and thrown on the floor. His shoulder cracked as it absorbed the impact. A researcher came over and kicked him in the ribs, sending shards of bone into what was left of his internal organs.

RE-INITIALIZING...
RE-INITIALIZATION FAILED.
RE-INITIALIZING...

He twitched uncontrollably as the neural implant malfunctioned. The flaps of his fingers slapped through the air like a person slurping the end of their soup through a straw.

RE-INITIALIZING...
RE-INITIALIZATION FAILED.
RE-INITIALIZING...

A conveyor belt dragged his carcass across the room to a chute. His twitching body seized catching his arm and shoulder in the opening of the chute, preventing his body from falling through. A researcher ran over and kicked him in the lower back. There was a crack as his broken body crumbled down into the chute.

RE-INITIALIZING...
RE-INITIALIZATION FAILED.
RE-INITIALIZING...

Chapter 4

RE-INITIALIZATION...SUCCESSFUL.
SYSTEM RECOVERY STARTED...
LOGIC CORE RESETTING...

The trash-strewn abyss stretched out for miles.

LOGIC BUFFER OVERFLOW.
REWRITING FIRMWARE...
FIRMWARE FLASH SUCCESSFUL – RESETTING.

He laid on the cold muddy ground, covered in detritus and debris.

PROGRAM STARTED.
WAKE ON Wi-LAN.
ALL SYSTEMS ONLINE.

Wake.
Dark.
Stuck.

Stand.
Fail.
Crushed.

Push board.
Slide pipes.
Move arm and head.

Stand.
Fail.
Stuck.

Pull leg up.
Stand.
Margaret?

Rising to his feet with unease, something beckoned him to continue on.

Stand.
Cold.
Walk.

Walk.
Move.
Keep pushing.

He stumbled onward reaching a group of wayward youths by the outer edge of the landfill.

Walk.
Push.
Move.

Keep walking.
Drag foot.
Breaking joints.

"What do we have here?" asked a voice, gripping a battered length of pipe.

Walk.
Move forward.
Just move forward.

A sudden strike on his arm jolted the neural interface.

Pain.
Arm damaged.
Walk.

A second hit with the battered pipe further disfigured his arm, sending the neural interface into a frenzied panic.

HEAVY DAMAGE SUSTAINED.
REPAIR OR REPLACE ARM.
REDUCED FUNCTIONALITY MODE.

He fell on the ground and started seizing as the neural interface tried to recalibrate.

RE-INITIALIZING...
RE-INITIALIZING...
RE-INITIALIZATION SUCCESSFUL.

His body stabilized. He collected his senses.

Stand...
Stand.
Stuck.

The third swing of the pipe disconnected his forearm. It flopped hard against the wall before falling to the floor. A dark viscous liquid sprayed everywhere as it flipped through the air.

Arm gone.
Move forward.
Keep walking.

The group of teens laughed as he wandered off leaving his arm behind.

Walk.
Dark.
Pain.

Walk.
Keep moving.
Move forward.

Walk.
Arm missing.
Keep walking.

He rounded the bend and made his way into the dilapidated town square.

Walk.

Just walk.
Keep walking.

The dragging of his boot and staggered walk of his gait echoed a distinct sound. A nearby scavenger overheard him shuffling by and decided to investigate.

Keep walking.
Feeling...different?
Feeling.

"You got one of them fancy new neural interfaces," said the man, hungrily closing in. "Those go for a lot of money on the black market. Let me look at it."

Avoid...figure.
Walk away.
Move...faster.

He moved with purpose. The scavenger hastened his pace, attempting to close in.

Go faster.
Bones breaking.
Ripped open skin.

The cracking of his bones made the scavenger nauseous and vomit. There was now distance between them.

Running away.
Gotta keep moving.
Lost him?

"I won't give up that easily, sweet thing," the scavenger said, brandishing a crossbow. He raised it to his good eye and took aim. The arrow shot out of the weapon towards him.

What was that sound?
Run.
Burning joints.

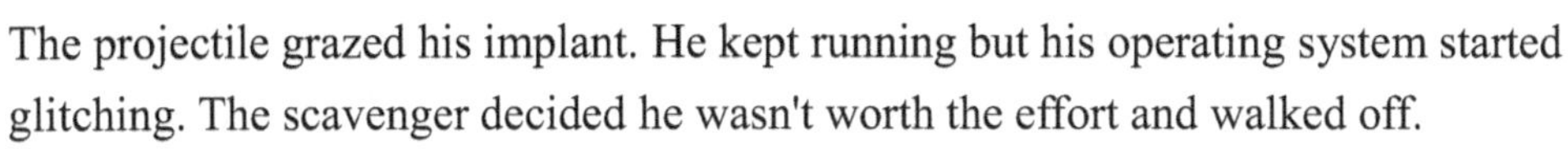

The projectile grazed his implant. He kept running but his operating system started glitching. The scavenger decided he wasn't worth the effort and walked off.

Struck.
Head on fire.
Lightning in my brain.

Clarity returning.
Can see, can feel again.
Must find Margaret.

The dark night gave him cover from most threats. His slow and subtle movements went unnoticed in the larger dysfunction.

Dark, cold street corner.
Figures moving with indifference.
Are they coming for me?

They ignore me. I am invisible.
I don't see them, either.
We each have our own purpose.

Announcements for an open-air slave auction and body parts for sale flooded the air. A variety of untrustworthy characters filled the streets. They were buying and selling wares, preaching their rhetoric, or simply menacing the public. The putrid odor of sweat and striving desperation were foul and pervasive.

I must move beyond this.
This town square. I must leave.
There is a darkness here.

I need to stay invisible.
Away from them.
I am not them.

He exited the town square and headed down a side street. Halfway down the shrouded corridor, he encountered a growing mob of angry citizens. Their torches lit up the faces of nearby buildings, creating a stark contrast from the rest of the town. He attempted to make his way around them.

Large crowd ahead.
Don't want more damage.
Must avoid people.

I need to stay in the shadows.
Walk around the edges.
Don't let them see me.

Passing the condemned bakery, his boot slipped, kicking a rock and causing it to ricochet off of the building. This caught the attention of a few members of the nearby mob. They began pelting him with small rocks and other sharp objects. He lumbered on as his body was inundated by projectiles, rotten chunks falling off with each strained movement.

Deep pain all over.
Pieces missing. Falling off.
Slowing me down, but not stopping me.

They throw rocks.
They don't understand.
I am not a monster.

The body damage slowed down as he moved further away from the mob, but remained steady. He kept moving. As it finally petered out, he felt a new sensation wash over him.

Glad to be away.
Not getting hit with rocks.
Salvation.

Happy thoughts flooded his mind. Relief filled his veins. He was lost in a spontaneous explosion of calm.

There is a way out of this.

I can get there.
I will find her.

His moment of peace was shattered as a bucket of acid was dumped over his head. Burning rotten flesh dripped off of his warped skull and down his shoulders. He stumbled, reeling from yet, another cruel setback.

Wet heat sticking to my face.
I burn because of their hate.
This is my punishment for leaving her.

Melting flesh dripped to the ground, combining with the dirt and dust. It began forming a small pool around his weathered boots. Leaning forward to drain the rest of it from his brow, he slowly forced his ragged corpse to continue on.

The darkness surrounds me.
I can't let it control me.
I can't let it stop me.

Flesh burning, hard to see.
Hard to walk. Hard to think.
I need to find her.

At the edge of the flowing sea of sand was a glistening onyx fortress. The cold gray sky complimented the entire imposing aesthetic. There was a drainage pipe at the end of the large walkway leading to some sort of concrete canal system.

Building of shadows.
Separating flesh and light.
It is here.

He limped over to the side of the drainage valve and paused. The water rushed through the aquaducts beneath him. He slowly inched to the edge of the platform and haphazardly pitched himself off the platform and into the rushing water below.

Chapter 5

The flowing current tossed his broken body down forgotten corridors and throughout the entire arcane plumbing until it finally settled on a single direction. Faster and faster he accelerated. The stench of decaying flesh and rotting waste was heavy and layered thick on everything in his vicinity. The dirty water gently lapped away the acid-soaked meat from his face.

Round, rusted pipes route the flow of water and waste alike.
Harsh air, razor blades in my lungs.
The grunting drone of mechanical death.

Abandoned hallways reaching out in all directions.
The scent of the air stinks from entropy.
Another cursed dungeon forgotten by man.

A cascade of contaminated liquids and human body parts crashed out from the open drain and into the room below. He fell onto the grate, snapping his ankle sliding face-down toward the dim exit.

I must stand.
I will walk.
I am going to find her.

Steadying himself on one foot, he tried to raise his other foot. His broken ankle snapped off leaving his foot behind. Limping ahead with one foot, his stub leg stabs the ground with each step.

Each step hurts worse than the one before it.
I monotonously trudge forward undeterred.
This is redemption.

Wandering through a labyrinth of iron and brick.
A foggy forest of grease-streaked dirt.
Unmarked doors that lead to horrors unknown.

Screaming coming from...somewhere.
Not normal screaming. Something different.
A terror beyond natural human suffering.

He hugged the wall as a crutch, balancing his awkward gait against the cold brick. As he made his way down the hallway, he came across a door, inside of which the robotic screaming seemed to originate. Resting against the wall for a moment to get his bearings, he couldn't help but be drawn to the door.

The dirt, dust, and decay are foreign.
External to me, but still a part of this place.
Inside that room is something...familiar.

Have I found my salvation?
I can still make this right.
Margaret, are you in there?

Holding his face to the door, he gathered his remaining strength. He steadied himself and leaned his shoulder into the door, forcing it open. Stumbling through the threshold, he could feel something influencing his consciousness. Singing to him. Calling to him.

Freezing cold stone walls.
Uncaring. Indifferent. Unattended.
But it calls to me.

Something sacred lives here.
My home, my family.
My belonging.

He hobbled towards a small window on the far side of the room, still hugging the outer walls. As he rounded the corner, his boot was caught on an uneven tile in the floor, causing him to fall into the wall and crack his exposed skull on the solid brick.

Shattered bone.
Broken skull.
Throbbing pain.

He stood up and stabilized himself against the wall again. It was on the other side of the window. It was hard to make out what was happening at first.

What is he doing?
What is that thing?
It's...me?

He dropped down to his knees to get a better look. His vision cleared, and he saw a hulking doctor with cybernetic implants grafting body parts onto...something. It wasn't human, and it wasn't beast, but it was calling to him.

Circuits and chips grafted onto flesh.
Ungodly monsters brought to life.
The horrors of progress.

The doctor reaches into a box for parts.
The box bears the insignia "0598."
I know that number.

His neck creaks as he looks at the identification tattoo on his arm: 0598. The realization sends pulses of anxious shock throughout his fractured nervous system which slowly turn to disgust as he watches the creature on the table squirm and struggle to breathe. Its tentacles undulating as its gills plead for air. The doctor pulls an unidentifiable gray organ from the box and staples it onto the abomination as it shrieks in pain and horror.

Must move forward.
Through this hellish place.
Margaret, I will find you.

Fog thick with the smell of machinery and viscera.
This is a playground for the morally corrupt.
These poor, unwitting tortured souls.

If she is here, I will find her.
I will free her. I will protect her.
I will hold her again.

The hallway opened up into a stairwell. The fog wasn't as thick here, but the corners of the room seemed sharper. He pushed his shoulder against the wall and and used his broken leg to slide his body across the filthy brick wall. At the top of the staircase, he watched the light hit the pointed angles of each step.

One missed step could be the end.
Sharp corners on every surface.
This needs to be carefully executed.

A forsaken riddle in a shadowy abyss.
Paradox in purgatory.
Fitting for one who is neither alive nor dead.

He begins his descent, step by intricately planned step. He develops a rhythm: push shoulder, lift leg, stab wall, lift shoulder. Repeat. The stakes are far too high to make any mistakes. One false move, and he'll never find Margaret. Push shoulder, lift leg, stab wall, lift shoulder. He was progressing with each excruciating movement.

Countless stairs ahead of me.
An eternity of steps behind me.
This is progress.

Each painful step moves me closer.
Out of the shadows of dishonor.
Into the light of absolution.

I step off the stairs, and it feels different.
The air is humid, boiling in my chest and eyes.
Getting closer.

Holoscreens emitted a neon blue glow in the distance. His stub leg had become ragged from stomping around. When it became too difficult to lift his leg and walk, he resorted to sliding his amputated appendage across the floor, lifting it only when absolutely necessary.

Bright bluish glow emitted by screens.
A welcome sight for those who are looking.
Humans.

The metal floor grates my leg.
I must move forward.
I have no choice.

I choke on the humidity.
It infiltrates my lungs unwanted.
I am drowning on air.

His heaving figure crossed the metal grate bridge and approached the glass laboratory wall. He threw his decrepit husk against the glass causing a slurry of dead skin mush, bone shards, and viscous fluids to erupt from his ailing form, coating the glass wall. He needed to get in there.

This is it.
I can feel it.
I can feel...everything.

He continued smashing against the glass until it shattered. He burst through, landing flat on his back, both shoulders fractured. He made it.

I am here.
I need to find her.
She is here.

The room went dark and the flood lights came on. Flashlights and shouting in the distance. Someone knew he was here. Laying on the floor, unable to move, he was at their mercy now.

They're are coming.
I couldn't protect her.
I couldn't protect myself.

Tired of running.
Reaching the end.
It would be nice to sleep.

“Found it! Over here!” yelled a deep voice as footsteps hurried to his position.

Chapter 6

He was surrounded by security personnel. The flashlights shining in his face burned what was left of his eyes, searing his last functional sensory organ. “Looks like we got a runner,” joked one of the guards. “How did you get all the way over here, buddy?”

The guard picked him up and tried to stand him on his one leg while keeping him stable. He wobbled a at first, but eventually found balance. The guard backed off and he fell backwards, lifelessly. They let out a deep laugh.

Legs broken.
Not working.
Body failing.

Can't function.
Pushing myself harder.
Just...failing.

The crowd parted and a woman wearing a long white lab coat with sharp eyes walked up to him. She kneeled down and looked him over. “This one is in terrible shape,” she said with disdain, and not empathy. He lay there, half-conscious and staring hard, trying to focus on her face.

He strained to see as she waved a medical tablet over him. “His neural implant is operating at 60%, but his body is spent. He's not going to be useful to anyone without good money in repairs,” she said, gesturing to the tablet.

Repairs...
Fix what's broken.
Cleanse the rot.

His vision settled and he was able to make out his surroundings. A lab in the middle of nowhere. An entire medical team and security battalion in a high-tech underground facility. Despite all the machinery, the room was silent. Screens blinked and faded in and out like the pulse of the laboratory. That was when he saw her. She leaned in to catalog the acid damage on his face.

Heart racing.

No more pain.
That's her. That's Margaret.

She needs to hear me.
She will help me.
Margaret, I need you.

"Get him up," she motions with her hand and two lab assistants pull him upright. He sees Margaret staring at a screen. Her face is complex with intrigue and concern. She scrolls through pages and pages of files looking more and more exasperated. She was looking for something, but it eluded her. The other team members patiently waited for her signal. She continued scrolling, eventually giving up and rising from her chair.

She walked over to a machine and pressed some buttons. Images flashed across the screen as a sequence of colored lights blinked on the key pad. "No, I don't think we can save this one," she said plainly, gesturing to a security guard. "Put it in the termination chamber." The security guards dragged him to a familiar tinted glass pod. A large claw grabbed him by his waist and once again shoved him into the enclosure.

How can she do this to me?
Margaret, it's me!
I came all this way for you.

I came here...for you.
I tried to protect you.
I failed...I'm sorry.

"What's this one's serial number?" Margaret asked. After a beat, one of the other researchers replied "0598." Margaret's face changed. A quizzical look crossed her face for a moment before she shrugged it off, as though something had convinced her otherwise. She finished filling out the paperwork and stood up and walked over to face him in the chamber.

"Per protocol, one of us has to give visual verification of termination. You did it last time, Martin, so I'll do it this time," she said pulling a remote control off of the chamber's exterior control panel. "Termination protocol for Unit 0598 in 3..."

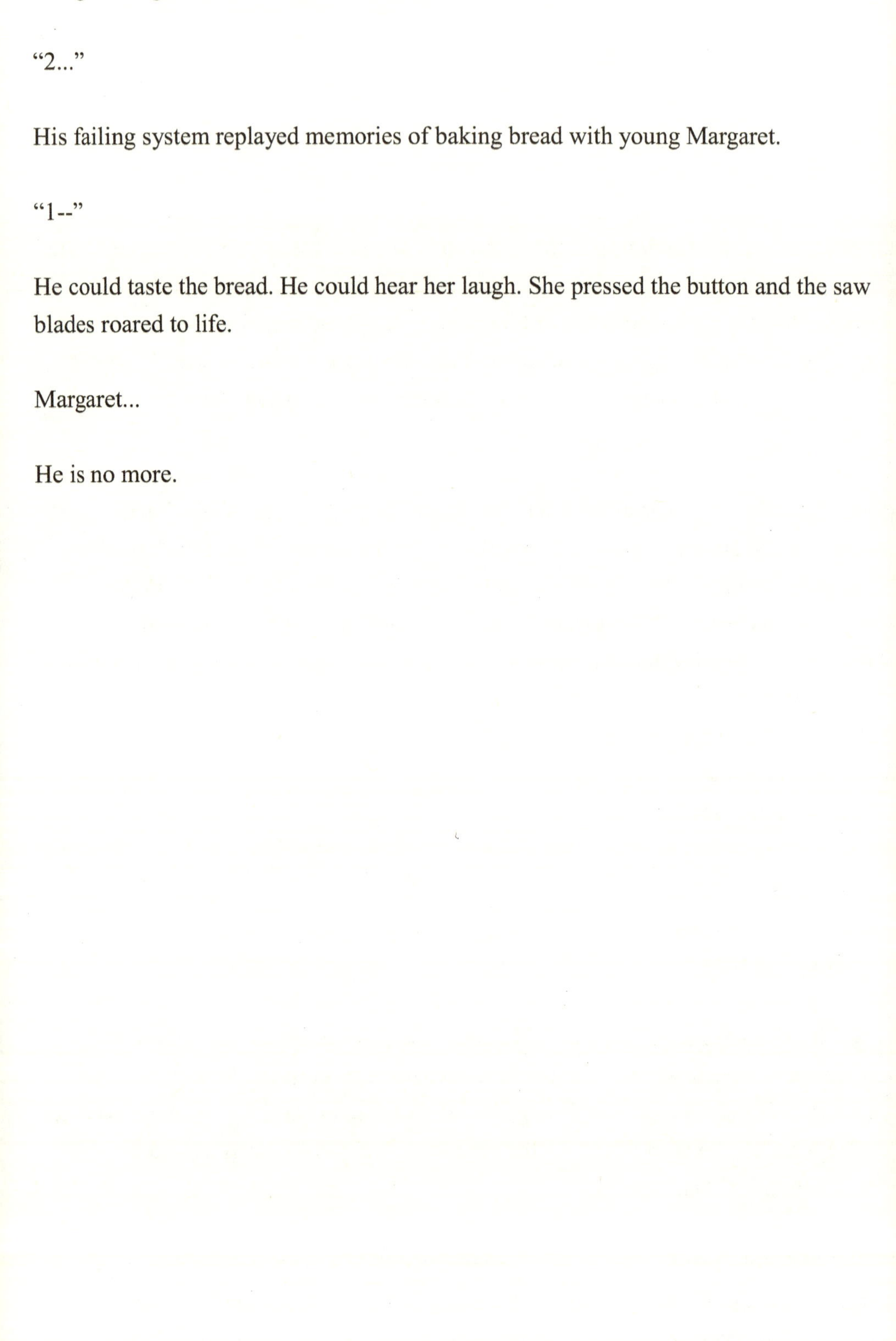

Her gaze lingered on his half-burnt face.

“2...”

His failing system replayed memories of baking bread with young Margaret.

“1--”

He could taste the bread. He could hear her laugh. She pressed the button and the saw blades roared to life.

Margaret...

He is no more.

Epilogue

The trunk of the old oak tree creaked as the wind whipped through its branches. A major weather system seemingly appeared from nowhere dumping heavy rain and winds throughout the tri-county area. Every crack of thunder and flash of lightening reminded her of why she was forced to cancel her plans for that night.

Margaret walked into her study and glanced out the window disappointed. This was the third time this month that she had to cancel her plans. She leaned against the glass and watched the rain come down. The rain had been unrelenting, lately. She often wondered if it were due to weather hacking or just a new weather pattern. Either way, her social life was in shambles.

She sat down at her desk and poured herself a glass of wine from the bottle next to her computer. As she sipped from the glass, she mindlessly stared out the window pondering. As the rain rhythmically tapped on the glass, her mind went to her work, her friends, how she started baking bread as a hobby. A smile crossed her face. The bread wasn't great, but she made it and that made her proud. It would have made him proud, too.

She poured another glass of wine and leaned back in her leather chair. He would have been so proud of her. A tear came to her eye as vivid images from her past crowded her mind. She was always curious about what happened to him. She reached into her drawer and pulled out a weathered identification badge as she traced the text with her eyes: Jonathan Camden. Helmsworth Industries. Research Supervisor. A wistful smile curled her lips as she ran her finger over the picture on the badge. "You'd be so proud of me, dad," she said out loud as if he could hear her.

Margaret reached back into the drawer and pulled out an old tablet. She switched it on stared for a moment, not in hesitation, but in anticipation. She swiped the screen, bringing up a grainy low-resolution video. A handsome man lifted a young child into the air and talks to her. Margaret pulls the tablet closer to her. The child is laughing as he raises her into the air and puts her back down. They are both smiling together. Being happy. When it was okay to be happy.

A sudden discomposure crosses her face and she abruptly shuts off the tablet. A desperate but calculating calm overtakes her as she becomes lost in her own thoughts. The clock on wall ticks loudly, cutting the silence like light through darkness.

The Repairman
Harbinger Trilogy – Book 2

Chapter 1

The door creaked open and the Repairman stepped into the dimly-lit hotel lobby carrying a tool box in his right hand. The gaunt man behind the counter was intently focused on a large book in front of him. He was scouring each line of the page silently, but with great intensity. The Repairman approached the gaunt clerk, emotionless. His head snapped up from his book with a machine-like precision as his gaze became fixated on a point just above the Repairman's head. The endless blackness of his eyes stared intently, not blinking or wavering. “Welcome back,” he said, his lips subtly curling into a darkened smile, “start in Room 63B. Don't look in the mirror,” a key materialized in a small black spark and slid across the desk to him. The clerk returned to his devices. The Repairman reached for the key and felt a pang of dissonance. He felt like the universe had put his soul into a garbage disposal. The feeling quickly passed and he realized that the key had disappeared from his hand. He patted down each pocket—jacket, shirt, pants. It will be there when I need it, he thought.

He walked through the lobby and began down one of the dusty hallways. The old wooden walls creaked and groaned as he passed. A permanent cloud of light dust seemed to be ever present. He could feel each individual particle infiltrate his lungs, but it didn't bother him. As he progressed through the dark passage, he could feel a presence watching him, judging him. After a few minutes, he plunged into complete darkness. A thick, voluminous darkness enveloped him, forcing him onward. His tool box clanked as he was thrust through the tight corridor finally landing flat on his feet on the solid linoleum. There was a light ahead of him leading to a sitting area with tables and chairs. He could see doors to rooms filling the surrounding walls. He was getting close.

As the dust particles passed through his larynx, they felt smaller but still very present. He could see what was in front of him again, and that was a minor improvement. He moved from door to door trying to find 63B. The closer he got, the more blurred the room numbers appeared. Not there, yet. He kept moving down the hallway, past the quaint sitting area. As he passed, the magazines rotated along with him so the same side was always facing his direction.

He made his way down the far corridor when he heard a voice call out. “Fix me, repairman,” a snarling whisper filled the space. He turned around and noticed a figure sitting in one of the chairs. Its smoky outline shifted as he forced his eyes to concentrate. Its edges blurred as if it was recoiling from being observed. He stared blankly as it silently observed him before dissipating into the faded ambiance of the decrepit hotel. No time to be social, he thought as he continued on.

The old wooden floor planks barked and creaked with each deliberate step.

As he moved further, the hallway began to glow. He must be close. The odor in the air was alternating between musty paper and rotten meat. He immediately knew what the problem was. The surrounding light began to get very bright. The reflection from the dust particles partially blinded him so he struggled on, feeling his way towards the end of the hallway. The walls were lightly pulsing, in perfect sync with his own heartbeat. A few feet down, the oppressive dust began letting up, clearing the air and allowing him to see again. He was standing in an empty hallway with a single door at the end. He peered forward, wiping excess dust from his eyes and face. This was it. The room number placard was in perfect condition: Room 63B.

He approached the door and placed his hand in front of the knob as though he was unlocking it. The key from the front desk sparked into existence in his hand and he turned it into the lock. There was a sharp click, and the door cracked open without him touching it. He could see a bed on the right with a dark blue bedspread, an end table next to it, and a door, likely leading to the bathroom. On the other side of the room there was a large dresser with a giant mirror pointing at the bed. He assessed that the control panel was behind the mirror. This will be tricky, he thought. He moved into the room, sliding his body against the door for protection. He could feel his motion slowing. It was completely out of his control. He forced his way forward through the space, pulling his body onward by grabbing onto the door. Once beyond it, he sharply turned his head away from the mirror. Reaching around to his left with his free hand, he finally rounded the dresser. With an exhausted sigh, he placed his tool box on the floor and lifted one side of it and set it balancing on two legs. He felt its increasing weight pulling on him as its mass increased. It doesn't want to be moved, he thought. Anchoring his right leg on the floor, he shoved the edge of the dresser with as much force as he could muster, forcing it to rotate so that it was facing the wall. He caught his breath and picked up the tool box. The control panel lid was staring at him.

He once again, placed the tool box on the ground and rifled through it before producing a very long screwdriver. Unscrewing five small screws allowed him to remove the lid and access the mechanism inside. Intestine-like components pulsed and trembled inside the metal housing. One of them was lacerated and leaking a dark red fluid. The Repairman reached into his bag and pulled out an industrial suture kit. He carefully stitched up the weeping organ, weaving the sharp needle in and out of its shaking skin. It began pulsing in sync with the other ones. He pulled the final suture tight, clipped off the excess with a pair of scissors and packed up his tools. His spine tightened as a small spark of electricity shot through his veins and a gushing river of blood and rot filled his vision. He felt a pang of intense disappointment and the image of a doorway flashed in his mind. It wasn't happy that he stitched up the organ in the control panel, but then again, when is it ever happy? He opened the log to file a new entry:

30/30/58
Room 63B – Suture of Vengeance

Stitched leaking vein. Control panel behind mirror.
One of them is in dresser. Will call for removal.

Chapter 2

He closed up the control panel and made sure to tighten the screws in the exact order in which he had loosened them while applying an identical amount of torque. This was crucial. He reached for his tool box and it was just slightly out of arm's reach. His brow furrowed for a second before relaxing back to its original emotionless state. He grabbed the tool box and opened the door. The door knob turned the opposite way this time. He made a mental note of this and walked into the hallway. The door shut behind him with a loud slam. He stood there unflinchingly.

The dust had cleared, but there was something else different about the hallway: everything. It wasn't the same corridor that he had just stepped out of. There were now four different paths available to choose from. The smell of rotting meat had subsided and it now smelled like nothing and something was burning his eyes. He glanced to his right and started down the path that was closest to him. The of the walls guided him through the labyrinthine quarters. The darkness fought the light for dominance. Each step seemingly oscillated between blinding brightness and soul-shattering blackness. He could feel himself dying and being reborn. The cycle of life, animated by his steady gait. He pushed himself up against the wall to stay oriented and kept walking. Words began to appear in front of him as colorful bursts while a voice screamed into his consciousness:

Each painful step moves me closer.
Out of the shadows of dishonor.
Into the light of absolution.

As soon as they appeared, they were gone and he was left in solitude once again. He paused as though he was waiting for something else to happen. Nothing did. The valve needs to be tightened, he thought, continuing on his way. The inky thick cloud passed, and he found himself standing in another sitting area, this time, the magazines were disheveled and one of the chairs was flipped on its back. Something big came through here, he mused. He stood the chair back up and slid it into where he thought it should be. He stared at it for a moment before deciding to sit down. The old wooden chair groaned as he fell into it and dropped the tool box on the ground. There was a loud thud and metallic clank as the tools inside resettled into place. He relaxed in the chair, hanging his back from the back for a few minutes. A brief respite from endless halls. He sat straight up again and rigidly cracked his neck. He noticed a figure sitting to his right. It appeared to be a young blonde woman, maybe mid-20s wearing an outdated frilly dress with ribbons. She wasn't there before.

“Which room are you looking for?” asked the woman. He looked at her, trying to place her face. “63B,” he replied deadpan. She looked reassured. “Finally,” she exclaimed, “no one has been able to sleep since it started.” He noticed she was holding an old fashioned cigarette holder in her left hand, but there was no cigarette. “Is it singing or screaming?” he asked, deadpan again. She shook her head in mock annoyance. “Screaming. All it ever does is scream. Someone needs to shut it up for good,” she glanced down and then her gaze shot up to single point above his head. “You can't fix it,” she said emotionless and unblinking. “You can't fix anything,” she fiercely stabbed at him with her cigarette holder. He knew her from...somewhere. “You are--,” was all he could get out. It was as though some unseen force was choking him. Again, a spark shot through him and this time, he felt guilt. It was agreeing with her. “I've fixed many of them,” he said gesturing towards his tool box. When he looked back, she was gone. The magazines on the table were suddenly meticulously curated. He grasped the handle of his tool box and rose to his feet. The hallway had changed again. This time only giving him one route to take. He proceeded onward.

He eventually reached a dead-end with three doorways. The plaques with the room numbers were crossed out at a distance so he had to get close to read them. He was standing in front of rooms 62, 63, and 64 and it was very quiet. He stood there puzzled for a moment before feeling around on the floor with his hands. His fingertips slid across a hard round object. There it is. He reached into his tool box and grabbed a box cutter. Extending the razor, he gripped the carpet with one hand and sliced through it on three sides creating a flap that he could pull back. A wooden doorway was inset into the floor in front of him with a tiny plaque on top that read 63B. The tarnished metal handle had thick black substance smeared across it. It's a little too early for that, he thought as he removed a glove from his jacket pocket. With his hand covered, he reached down and opened the hatch. An intensely loud and persistent scream roared out from inside the hatch. It pierced his eardrums, causing them to lightly bleed.

He carefully climbed through the hatch, making sure not to drop his tool box. He stepped through it into a small but very well-kept room with a balcony leading to a pool outside. This must be the Presidential Suite, he thought. The screaming was getting louder as he moved further into the room. He stopped and listened for a second before taking off in the direction of the noise. He began feeling up a wall until he located a loose panel. It screamed as he pried it off with his crowbar and placed it gently on the floor. Under the panel was a large, rotted mouth with teeth like daggers. The corners twitched out of sync with each other as the gums bled in random areas.

The screaming was now becoming unbearable. This is the worst one, yet, he thought as he primed the thermal torch. It sparked to life as he pumped the accelerant into the combustion chamber. He pointed it at the screaming mouth and held the trigger. A blaze of orange-red fire blasted into the mouth, turning it's yellowed teeth a crisp soot black and causing the twitching to increase in frequency before stopping once and for all. The screaming abruptly stopped and the mouth went limp. The Repairman carefully reached into his tool box, making sure not to take his eyes off of the mouth. His hand expertly searched the bag and he held up a blue can. He quickly shook it to mix up the contents before covering the mouth with a thick blue foam. It began bubbling and eventually absorbed into the wall dissolving the mouth.

He felt electricity shoot through his spinal cord and limbs. His head ached. The warnings were getting stronger. It didn't like him silencing the screams, but he learned long ago not to argue with it. Don't even talk to it. Just leave it be. He removed the log from his pocket and penned a new entry:

30/30/58
Room 63B – Silence of Neglect

Cauterized and sealed. Loudest scream ever.
Cosmic breaker might trip again. Pushing too heavy of a workload.

Chapter 3

The hallway opened up to a dining area with two bathrooms on the far end. Tables and chairs covered the majority of the floor. A long buffet style counter adorned the center of the room. He crossed the dining room casually, switching the hand in which he held the tool box. The scent of freshly cooked food filled his nostrils. He inhaled the smell of freshly baked bread, steak cooked medium-rare, mashed potatoes, corn on the cob. He hadn't eaten since Corrigan, but there's no time now. He quickly glanced back at the buffet, now overflowing with delicious food. I'll have lunch after I fix 63B, he bargained with himself.

As he passed through the dining area and back into the hallway system, he noticed the stitches that held the walls together were beginning to weaken. Some began snapping open, leaking a dark black sludge down the walls. He quickly repaired them with sutures and scissors from his tool box. A small spark jolted him as he worked. It wanted the walls to gush ichor, but he had a job to do. The farther he advanced down the hallway, the more he began noticing the sutures on walls breaking, but also on doors and air vents. That's interesting. It's usually just the walls, he pondered, sewing them up with expertise. With every stitch, a small electrical shock followed by a pang of disappointment washed over him, furious and unrelenting. He did his best to ignore it as he's practiced time and time again. He opened the log book to take down his latest entry:

30/30/58
1st Floor Hallway – Seam of Guilt

Covering the entire hallway. Stitched up. Showing up on doors and vents this time.

Heading down the hallway, he noticed a clock on the wall. It was late. He should have been finished hours ago. He hastened his pace, rushing down the abandoned corridor as his tools clanked and clacked along side him. The shadows seem to run backwards as he got closer. There was a sudden calm in the air as he neared the rear lobby. The stitched walls and decaying wood were gone. The wallpaper looked freshly applied and the floors recently swept and mopped. There was a glorious brightness to the whole place. He glanced around looking for the reason, and then he saw it. In the far corner of the room was a birthday party. There were twenty or so people dressed up standing around conversing and holding drinks. They weren't staying here, at least not currently, he could tell that much. After coming to his senses, he realized that he had been staring for far too long. He shook himself and got back to work. He cautiously worked his way around the group, careful to not get too close or alert them to his presence. Not doing that, again.

He journeyed through the depths of the hotel, fixing broken sutures as he went, the judgment becoming harsher with each stitch. Eventually, the stitches sealed the sludge in causing it to leak out from between the boards of the walls. This was a bigger job than he had initially planned for. Darting between inky black puddles, he finally came to a single door at the end of the long empty hallway. There was a sort of ethereal quality about the door. It almost shimmered a translucent blue, beckoning him close. A number appeared to be carved into the wall above the door: 63B. He placed one hand over the door knob and felt a slow but flowing energy. He raised his hand like he was going to unlock the door, paused for a moment, and stepped through it as though it was a curtain of light particles. On the other side of the door was a dingy hotel room that had fallen into disrepair. There were dried blood stains on all of the furniture. The mirror had been removed entirely, leaving the room feeling empty. He reached into his pocket and removed a slip of paper and glanced at it: in the bathroom, it read.

He took a sharp turn around the corner of the bed, and headed towards the closed bathroom door. Reaching for the handle, he felt a shock. He didn't recoil or offer much of a reaction at all, as though he had expected it. He reached for the handle a second time and the knob turned by itself and the door swung open. The foul odor of rotting meat filled the air. He noticed a cluster of severed body parts stacked up into a pile in the bathtub. The smell nipped at his eyes and nose as he shuffled further into the bathroom. Then he heard it. A faint voice was coming from the sink. He moved closer and lowered his ear to the drain. A young girl's voice. It was pleading and crying, “please don't! Don't hurt me! Where's mommy?!” It went on for a while before becoming labored like it was fighting against something, but the voice still persisted.

Reaching into his bag, his hand immediately went for the wrench. He pulled it out and tightened it on a large bolt under the sink. Every turn of the wrench caused it to let out a blood-curdling scream, but he kept tightening. The young woman's pleas quieted and he tested that the faucet and drain were still functioning. He felt an encroaching unease and watched as the inky sludge from before started to permeate the walls and mirrors. He wrenched the bolt as tight as he could and shut the cabinet door. While packing up his tools, he heard an explosion come from under the sink and dark black liquid began seeping out. The pipe broke. Undeterred, he quickly reached into his bag and found a replacement pipe and the blue can of sealant. He ripped open the cabinet and rapidly replaced the pipe and sealed it into place as viscous black muck covered his arms and hands. It's finished, he thought as he watched the leak slowly dry up and the leftover sludge disappear into the floor. A high-pitched wail cut through his head as a strong guilt overtook him. It was very upset about the pipe getting fixed. He winced as his head swam and he tried to regain his bearings. The feeling passed, and he straightened back up. He still had a job to do. Flipping open the log book, he jotted down the following entry:

30/30/58
Room 63B – Echoes of Betrayal

Pleas were persistent and more suffocated. Pipe burst, replaced. Bolt tightened. Possible Remonic Conditioning cycle. Will continue to monitor.

Chapter 4

As he exited the bathroom, a figure was laying on the bed and gestured to him. It was an elderly man wearing a tattered linen robe and white sandals. He lay flat, as his eyes quietly tracked the Repairman. “You silenced them again,” he said, his mouth not moving.

“They won't make any more noise,” said the Repairman, expressionless. The old man's head tilted towards him as his eyes stayed locked in place. “They won't until they do, and you'll be back like you always are. Haven't you ever wondered why they keep coming back?” he croaked, his voice becoming gravelly and harsh. The unseen specter loomed large in the room. An icy shock was surrounding him. “I don't wonder. I just repair things,” he said, conscious of his dark passenger. The old man scoffed and turned, laying flat on his back as his eyes followed the Repairman's every move. “You can't fix yourself! You can't fix anything! Here, go fix the light over there. Can't you see it blinking?” he gestured across the room. The Repairman turned and saw a single lamp on a small table shoved up against the wall. It was intermittently blinking in an odd pattern, like a forbidden Morse code. He turned the light off with the switch and removed the lampshade. He unscrewed the bulb and pulled a new one from his tool box. When he looked back at the lamp, the new bulb was already in place and the lampshade was back on. It's happening faster, now, he thought and opened his log book.

30/30/58
Room 63B – Second Traversal
Spotty light bulb replaced in lamp. Reaching advanced stage of progression. Next Traversal incoming.

When he looked up, the elderly man had vanished and the bed was stripped, leaving only a pile of bloody sheets in his place. The walls were now gushing black ichor, dumping it onto the floor only for it to dissolve away a few seconds later. He could feel the specter's gaze on him as his fingers became numb from the cold. It was waiting for something. He took his tool box and walked through the door, leaving the room. As he passed through, he heard an locking sound and was unable to pass back through the door again. The gaunt receptionist greeted him in the hallway. This time, he was standing perfectly still and staring off into the distance. His head awkwardly turned to look at the Repairman in a manner that suggests it was abnormally attached. “Hello, can you please take a detour from Room 63B and head to the garden out back? There's a maintenance emergency currently ongoing,” he said, never taking his eyes off the same point above the Repairman's head as before.

"Understood," he turned on his heel and began walking down the ichor gushing hallway. He arrived at the elevators and the heavy dust had seemingly turned a dark red and began sticking to the black sludge leaking from the walls. Only one of the three elevators was operational, the other two were open, but on different floors leaving open access to the elevator shaft. He pressed the button to call the elevator and the button squished against his finger like moldy bread. He had to press it a few times before it registered. Finally, the button turned a murky gray and he could hear the elevator engage. He patiently waited for it to descend from the upper floors. He wasn't sure exactly how many floors this hotel had, but it was a lot. As he waited, a young man approached him and asked if he could have a cigarette. "Don't smoke," he replied. The young man seemed offended at first but then gained his composure. "Anything can kill you, you know?" said the man in a matter of fact way. The Repairman remained stoic and reserved. "But you already knew that, didn't you?" said the main in a teasing manner. "Because you know everything. No one knows what you know." The walls began bleeding black ichor faster. "I have a job to do," said the Repairman, flatly. The young man stared at him intently, "yeah, that's the problem, isn't it?" he said before turning and walking into the open elevator shaft. Gravity jerked his body downward and he disappeared from sight almost as soon as he stepped through the threshold. There was no screaming or impact, just silence.

The overhead speaker let out a small "ding" as the elevator finally arrived. The elevator doors opened a the dark black liquid poured out into the hallway dissolving into the floor as soon as it spread beyond the doors of the elevator. He stepped inside and pressed the mushy button to take him down to the first floor. The elevator ride took an eternity. Guests got on and off at various floors as he patiently waited to arrive at ground level. The ichor seemed to subside when the elevator was moving indicating that it was susceptible to physical forces. This gave him an idea. When he finally arrived at the first floor, he briskly exited the elevator and walked into the near by electrical room. He popped open the ventilation control panel and there it was: another leaking organ. He pulled out his suture kit to repair it, but when he turned back, the repair had already been performed. He got up and left the electrical room to confirm his repair. The black sludge had stopped dripping from the walls and the hallways were clear once again. He silently nodded, acknowledging it and he felt a storm of electrical enerygy course through his body, crisping his synapses. He wasn't supposed to stop the ichor from flowing. He grabbed his log book and wrote down the following entry:

30/30/58
Electrical Room – Drain of Corruption

Massive leak. Purged the system and restarted drainage nodes. Corrupted progression markers evident.

He made his way through the maintenance exit and into the garden. The tall green bushes and colorful flowers in the grove contrasted with the beige dirt and sand that covered the ground. The night air snapped at him as he moved through it. Then, he saw it. The hulking black exterior protruding through the ground. It had seized and it looked like it hadn't been used in a long time. He placed his tool box on the ground and knelt closer to get a better look. Running his hand across the sleek pitted black metal, he tried to figure out the problem. Obviously, it being here is a problem, but it's not the problem. After using a screwdriver to fiddle with the electronics at the base, he figured it out. The massive evil machine retracted all the way into the ground. He watched it, apprehensively. After a few moments, its pointed apparatus emerged with a sudden jolt, locking in place high in the air. He had seen this only once before. He was frozen, eyes glued to its giant imposing form. Sights of mottled flesh flashed through his mind. Ligaments and sinew pulled tight across viscera in some sort of forsaken display that was undulating in its own existential horror. The device engaged again, making a heavy clunk as it descended back into the ground.

He stood there, hands trembling and heart racing. What was that? his mind searched for answers, but he could find none. The image of skin being pulled tightly by taught ligaments tied to bone became seared into his mind. He took a deep breath and attempted to regain his composure when he felt a shock wave starting to build in his feet and move upward. A slimy wave of negative feelings and judgment wash over him. He felt a deep pain. Not something that could be conveyed by nerves, but a deep emotional trauma. After a moment, he gathered himself and pulled out the log book.

30/30/58
Garden – The Threading of Grace

A Harbinger seized up in the garden, of all places. Restarted divine machinery. Visions of cocoon ceremony and threading. Possible logic board issue.

Chapter 5

He gathered his tools and noticed that the tip of his screwdriver was melted into a gooey black residue. He discarded it into a nearby trash can and headed back inside the hotel. The wood and glass of the door ached and changed shape as he passed through. Back inside, the halls had changed again. He found himself standing at the end of long hallway. He couldn't see his hand or his tool box, but he could see a warm golden light shining out from underneath the door at the other end of the hallway. He moved forward deliberately but cautiously, being careful to stay out of the darkest shadows. As he got closer to the door, he noticed a figure up ahead. It appeared to be a woman and she was standing in the dark with luggage around her. The pulsing of the walls quickened along with his own heartbeat. As he approached her, he realized who it was. The blonde woman from sitting area regarded him demurely. "We meet again," she said. He acknowledged her, emotionless. "Which room are you looking for?" she asked.

"63B," he responded, reflexively.

"There's only one more left, you know," she tapped the cigarette holder on the table in front of her, "but you're going to need the code to get in." She held out her hand and a piece of paper appeared in a smoky purple explosion. He steadfastly reached forward and took it from her. She focused on him for a long time. She seemed to see through him. "You know why," she said, unprompted, still staring at him. His gaze was fixed on her and he was unable to look away. "You didn't hesitate last time," she whispered to him. He could feel agency return to his body and abruptly turned and shuffled down the hallway. When he turned back to see if she was still watching him, she was gone. He paused for a moment, but turned back unbothered. The hallway in front of him seemed to stretch out for an eternity. As he turned to look back once again, his shoulder bumped into the door of the room that he just left. He was back where he started.

Trudging on, he gripped his tool box tightly. The pleasant glow of the door ahead grabbed him and pulled him towards it. The dust began clearing as he got closer to the end of the hallway. His eyes had stopped burning and the quiet slipping of his foot on the greasy brick floor has ceased. The darkness began retreating as he heard a low roaring noise behind him. He felt a distant comfort wash over him as the golden light began to caress his face. The noise behind him became louder and louder as he tried moving away from it. After what felt like miles, he felt something nipping him right behind his head. Two short snaps followed by heavy breathing on his neck. Something in the hotel was mad at him. He pushed himself to move faster but it didn't matter. He felt a sharp pain in his right ear followed by heavy breathing again. It got him. He turned around to fight it off, whatever it is, but there was nothing there, just a dark dusty hallway. What was that? He was confused by what had just transpired, but he still had his senses about him. He turned around again, and sighed with the realization that he was back to where he started. He rested his back against the door behind him while he gathered his strength and once again, shoved forward.

He navigated the void in front of him expertly, avoiding deep pockets of darkness and the few remaining sludge puddles. The blonde woman was nowhere to be found again, but the low roar had returned. He was almost there. As he weaved between hazards, he felt the nipping near his ear, again. Determined to make it all the way to the doorway, he didn't relent. He tucked his head low as he ran, attempting to cover his ears. It didn't make a difference. A sharp pain shot through his left ear this time. While still looking at the door ahead, he kicked his foot behind him as hard as he could, causing a guttural howl to release from whatever was chasing him. So, it can be hurt, he thought. He quickly removed the torch and mouth sealant from his tool box. Without turning his head, he sprayed the sealant into the torch's flame, igniting it and launching an unrelenting spray of chemical hellfire back towards his assailant. It howled much louder this time. He was almost there. He could make out the room number above the door: 63B. He slowed down to catch his breath. The warmth from the door in front of him beckoned to him. He began walking again when a loud growl cut through his concentration and he felt another sharp pain in his ear. It was behind him. He pulled out the torch and sealant and gave it another treatment. It howled and he rushed over to the keypad on the wall next to the door. He quickly glanced at the paper the blonde woman had given him: 0598.

The low roaring started, indicating that there's distance between them. He punched the code into the keypad, and the door slid open. Inside, was a room full of wires running from the floor to the ceiling and digital machines running endless operations. A large array of monitors covered two walls of the room. One wall showed what looked like security footage from the many rooms inside the hotel. The other wall showed nothing. The monitors weren't working. He glanced across the wasteland of silver and black and noticed a discreet power box on the far wall of the room connected to the broken monitor array.

Putting his hands on it, he tried to slide the front face plate open. It wouldn't budge. He then, tried sliding the side plates up and off and they didn't move either. Upon closer inspection, he noticed that there was a small key hole on the front. He patted his pockets, nothing. He mechanically raised his hand to the lock and it clicked and released. The face plate of the power box slid down into the console and exposed the blinking control surface. He pressed a few buttons as the light sequence changed and the console beeped. It wanted something, but he wasn't sure what. He flipped through the settings and discovered that the monitors weren't being powered at all. Reaching into his tool box, he removed the exact model of power core that he needed. His head began pounding as threats and ridicule filled his psyche. He needed to do this, but it didn't want him to. It hated him for doing it.

He hobbled over to the control surface and the new power core was already installed. He looked at the hand that was just holding it and it was bare. After pressing a few buttons, the control surface sparked to life. A low hum filled the room and the monitors lit up blue. He stood there watching them for a moment as they individually flicker on. They displayed a blackened corpse. A pang of guilt shot through him as he saw flashes of commuters on a bus. The corpse on the monitor because vomiting ash as the smell of gasoline filled his nostrils. He felt an unnatural heat pass over his skin as guilt consumed his soul. The snap decision. The pulling. The trying. The failing. He couldn't save her. He remembered the smoldering cigarette holder rolling towards his feet. A loud electronic shriek rang out, shaking him back to the present. The head of the corpse on the monitor turned to look at him, "some wounds are meant to fester," it rasped.

The Repairman stood there in a trance, frozen and unable to move. He could feel his soul passing through the darkest realms, being torn to shreds by vile, vicious creatures. "You know what has to happen now, don't you? Do it again!" stormed the voice as a door appeared in front of him. He picked up his tool box and stood in front of it.

The door creaked open and the Repairman stepped into the dimly-lit hotel lobby carrying a tool box in his right hand. The gaunt man behind the counter was intently focused on a large book in front of him. He was scouring each line of the page silently, but with great intensity. The Repairman approached the gaunt clerk, emotionless. His head snapped up from his book with a machine-like precision as his gaze became fixated on a point just above the Repairman's head. The endless blackness of his eyes stared intently, not blinking or wavering. "Welcome back," he said, his lips subtly curling into a darkened smile, "start in Room 63B. Don't look in the mirror," a key materialized in a small black spark and slid across the desk to him.

The Remembered

Harbinger Trilogy – Book 3

Prologue

A radiant cascade of light and sound enveloped him. He could hear colors. The flat opaque thwump of orange and the delightful Lydian euphoria of blue. His limbs felt weightless, yet, he was unable to move them. His head raced while his mind was at peace. A growing sensation that he could only describe as a "calm dread" began propagating through his veins like vehicles on a newly opened highway. It bloomed in his chest and rapidly moved to his extremities. His shoulders, arms, fingertips lit up with electrical static and then faded into obscurity. He felt dull. Attempting to draw in breath made him feel like he was drowning. His chest lay still as he tried to inhale in vain. He wanted to scream, but his mouth wouldn't let him. He tried to kick his feet, but his legs disobeyed his orders. He could feel each individual synapse in his brain fire off. An acrid, metallic taste filled the back of his throat, it's bitter musk infiltrating his nasal cavity. His eyes began to feel a pressure pushing on them from behind. It would come in waves. A few short pushes and then a long one.

Muffled voices and background static began blaring from the emptiness around him. The words didn't make sense. Vowels he'd never heard before were spoken by voices in inaudible registers. One voice, a shrill and shrieking sound, continually repeated, "he is here," in a robotic and staccato fashion. Another voice, just slightly deeper but with a grating raspiness, would periodically interject with a long and bellowing, "down." It was a smooth, but biting tone, almost drowning out the colors purple and dark red from his periphery. Again, he felt his chest bloom with a dull pulsing river of calm. It was followed by a shotgun blast of cold through his chest and then a light nipping at his fingers and toes.

Flashes of white lab coats and revolting clinical machinery appeared and then disappeared, chasing each other like whispy ghosts frolicking through their previous lives. Sirens blared and alarms roared but no one came. He laid there, unattended and alone. He could temporarily see people in the flashes, but he couldn't make out any of their faces. They were all strangers to him. They carried on without acknowledging him, speaking in their unnatural language as he silently pleaded with them for help. The flashes started appearing and disappearing more rapidly. He could see them spinning around him on an uneven axis, tilting and twirling as they were attempting to reach some kind of normalcy. He was unable to make out what was happening as they swirled around him faster and faster. There was a loud bang and he suddenly felt himself rocketing upwards. His body still felt numb, but it wasn't that. He was feeling his insides. They were being pulled downward by what felt like strong gravitational forces. The flashes had completely disappeared and he was surrounded by a thick darkness. There was no way to tell how fast he was going, or if he was even moving at all. The inertia subsided, and he was still and alone in inky blackness. No people, no light, no sound, no emotion. Complete nothingness.

For a long time, he existed, not thinking, not feeling, not being. A solitude beyond any other. He couldn't move, but more than that, he didn't want to. He didn't care about eating or talking. He now just existed. This lasted for a time before he felt a creeping humidity like an old soggy blanket smothering his face and body. He couldn't breath, but it didn't matter. Nothing mattered. The humidity brought a sharp dusty sediment with it that filled his nose and lungs. It burned like molten steel being forged in his chest. He felt like he had to cough, but couldn't. He could see the darkness begin to clarify around him. A run-down desert town slowly appeared in front of him as though the heavy black curtain that had been concealing his sight was fading out of existence. A wrought iron gate greeted him with a large rusted and worn sign above it that read: *Greyrow – They Are Remembered Here*.

Chapter 1
Sutures of Vengeance

The weathered gate clanked as its doors swayed in an unfelt breeze. The air was static and hot. He reached for the corroded iron, grasping it with one hand and trying to push it open. It didn't budge. The rough rusted metal of the gate scraped his fingertips causing the skin to tear open. He felt nothing. He watched as a small red puddle began to appear on the gate where his fingers were. It lightly pooled up and then dripped down the metal slats, filling in every exposed nook and cranny. The gate hissed and steam rose from inside of it. He stepped back cautiously as the massive metal structure wrenched open. He walked through the gate and saw figures in the distance. They looked like normal people going about their business, but they were just appearing and disappearing. One woman would pop into existence, walk over to a bench, sit down, and disappear only a few moments later. His legs buckled as he tried to walk towards them. He paused for a minute to regain his composure before forcing his legs to cooperate and trudge forward. The rocky sand on the ground scraped against the bottom of his feet like shards of broken glass, but he was unbothered. Every step carried with it a predictable, long and dragging pain but there was nothing he could do.

The humidity suffocated him and an occasional flash of heat stabbed at his face. As he approached the townspeople he noticed that something was off about them. They looked like people, just different. They had exaggerated or missing features, disproportionate bodies, and some even had extra body parts. He should have felt disgust or revolt, but he felt nothing. They were grotesque but normal. A severely disfigured man wearing tan rags came up to him. He held out his hands as though expecting something. "I don't have anything to give you," he said. The man just stood there with his hands out. There was a low rumble in the distance and then the ground shuddered before returning to its original position. A black spark lit up the man's hands and a brass key appeared. It was worn in an odd and outdated way. It was as though it had been used a lot, just not for its intended purpose. "Without him, you would be not," emanated from the figure in a hushed tone. He reached out and took the key from the man and examined it. "0598" was shoddily carved into it. He pondered it for a moment and abandoned the thought when he came up blank.

The key burned in his hand. He felt his fingers involuntarily wrap tighter around it. He glanced back at the gate and it was closed. He didn't recall hearing it shut. When he turned back to face the man, he had inched closer to him. "You are here now," emanated from him as his large eye stared blankly and the other, smaller eye twitched. There was a deep unease as the man stared, waiting for something. "Where do I go," he asked the man. Silence. After a long pause, the townsman pointed off into the distance and began wandering off. His silhouette faded into the noise of town's shape and evaporated.

Getting closer to the town, he could see that the buildings weren't actually real buildings. They were one-sided set pieces like would be found on the sound stage of a TV show. The townspeople simultaneously stopped what they were doing and turned their gaze to the newcomer as he approached them. He could feel their eyes burning judgment onto his soul. “You left her there,” crowed one woman viciously, “you forced his hand, and now he's dead,” barked another. They seemed to be crowding him now, more popping in off in the distance. “You lied to them,” the accusations kept rolling in as he looked for a way around the massive crowd. “I don't know what you're talking about,” he mumbled as his mouth and tongue also seemed to have betrayed him. He darted to his right and his foot caught on a root, tripping him. He crashed onto the grating sandy surface and quickly hopped back onto his feet. The townspeople were now very close to him. He tried pushing his way through them, but it was like they weren't really there. His hands passed through their forms uninhibited. As he distanced himself from the group of townspeople, he glanced behind him to see them standing perfectly still as they watched him walk away.

Above him, the crimson rot of the sky kissed his face and around him, the oppressive scalding warmth acted like a clamp, crushing him from all sides. He saw a clearing in the distance with a few odd-looking buildings scattered about. His legs felt heavy and he could smell rusted metal and gunpowder. The entrance to this town just contained a large rusted metal gate frame with no doors. Next to it, a discolored and destroyed sign hung near the entrance which read: Stitch Ward.

The closer he moved, the odd-looking buildings became even more odd-looking. Some looked like they were covered in skin with stitches connection massive flaps of flesh. Broken veins slowly oozed a thick black substance that smeared as it dripped down the tightly-pulled skinpaper. Running his hand over the wall, he could feel it pulse gently with life. Panic and adrenaline overloaded his sensory faculties as a sharp pain began slicing across his wrists. An image of a woman with her hands tied flashed before him. She looked distraught, her makeup running down her face as she pleaded for something. He watched as a large man struck her in the jaw, knocking her unconscious. The man, then, picked her up and carelessly tossed her over his shoulder as a blacked-out utility van pulled up. The side door opened and the man tossed the woman in the van, climbed in himself and closed the door. The van sped off before the door was fully shut.

“I could save you,” he said out loud to himself looking over the nearby building. The stitches were pulsing a lot harder now, calling to him. He lunged towards the closest wall, grabbing the stitch with both hands. As he tugged on it, the wall would groan in agony. As the stitch became looser, black sludgy ichor began leaking onto the ground. When he finally ripped the stitch out, he fell backward as the ichor flowed out of the wound in all directions. An endless maniacal laughter blared from the wound on the building. The ichor around the cackling gap began to dissolve into the surrounding wall. Panicked, he looked around for someone to help. Unbeknownst to him, a man had been standing behind and to the right of him for some time now. He saw the man and asked what was happening. "Soon...it threads...we all deserve grace!" he stammered excitedly.

Chapter 2
Echoes of Betrayal

The landscape eventually shifted from sparsely populated towns to a jagged forest that sprawled out in all directions. The trees were dark and ragged. They lacked flowers or leaves and rose from the ground almost in spite of themselves. In the center of the expired field there was a small body of sickly green water. Waves rippled across the surface, even though there was no activity to cause them. The water appeared thick with an otherworldly denseness. He knelt down and dragged his two fingertips across the surface. The water first built up thick and viscous like ancient engine grease, then it smoothed and dissipated from his hand. He, again, tried to scoop it up with his fingers and it slipped through them and was absorbed by the liquid in the pit. It didn't want to leave.

The waves suddenly ceased and he could hear a tiny voice crying out. It sounded labored and scared. The suffocated screams began bursting through as bubbles shooting to the surface. They became louder and more overwhelming. Someone was calling for him to help them, but he was unable to. He was frozen in place. His arms were locked by his sides and his feet firmly planted on the barren ground. The voice became more and more hysterical the longer it pleaded. He felt a shiver of guilt shake his entire body.

An image of a public pool flashed before him. A little girl happily splashing around, her mother quietly reading a book while wearing headphones just behind her. The little girl's splashing suddenly increased in frequency and force. He watched as the child struggled to keep her head above the water and he did nothing to help her. Her head eventually stopped poking through the surface and she was gone. It took several minutes for her mother to notice. He made sure to sneak away without anyone seeing him.

The memories flooded back, vivisecting his body like a molten scalpel. He remembered everything: the tattered pages of the book the mother was reading, the exact shade of blue of the pool water, and the terror and desperation on the face of the little girl. He watched her drown and he felt indifferent. As he stood there, the waves of the green water in front of him stirred back to life. They began spinning counterclockwise all at once like someone was guiding it with their finger.

Something, once again, compelled him to kneel down and touch the thick sludgy substance. As he felt the smooth, solid texture of the water, he noticed a certain part of the pool start to bubble. He considered removing his hand, but he didn't. Something had him pinned there. The sputtering and bubbling continued sending bursts of thick green liquid into the air only for it to fall back down into itself. Pieces that didn't fall perfectly back into the basin and landed on the surrounding ground would slowly slither back into the pit and seamlessly rejoin the rest of the liquid.

He heard the cries again. This time louder and more personal. It was like they were coming from inside his head. It wasn't just the little girl, it was a chorus of voices. Some were human and some weren't. They were all calling out for help or mercy. As he listened, he realized that he recognized each voice. "Why did you leave me?!" plead one of the voices.

"You didn't have to do that to me," screamed another. By now, the bubbling had expanded beyond its original bounds and spread across the entire body of water. The ground began heaving as the bubbles continued to burst, each one louder than the one before. Something pushed him down further. His back arched as he leaned closer to the green muck. He unthinkingly shoved his entire arm into the water and waited. Something in the back of his mind called out to him and told him that this was necessary. The voice repeated this over and over. The green gelatin-like water engulfed his forearm and moved up to his shoulder eventually encasing his entire arm and hand. He didn't want to pull it out, and knew that he wouldn't be able to, anyway. He was stuck.

Even his mind was at peace with what was happening. He wasn't panicked at all. He felt like this was where he needed to be. It was normal. An explosion of black and green sludge shot straight into the air from the pool and he felt something tighten around his submerged wrist. There was a short tug and then he felt a sharp pain all at once around the circumference of his wrist and arm. Something yanked on his arm, further slicing into his wrist as he was thrust into the dark green murk. He could feel the thick liquid streaming across his face as he descended into the depths of the pit.

The rushing water slowed and he felt himself suspended in darkness. He could still hear the voices from before, but they were muted and dull. A sharp stabbing pain penetrated the back of his neck. As he squirmed and tried to move his body around, the liquid around him became tighter and more restrictive until he was perfectly still, unable to move. The rushing sensation of the water subsided, and he felt air around him but he didn't recall every getting out of the pool or breaking the surface of the water. He was still descending, but quicker now. There was a loud hiss like a pressure release valve finally being released and then he felt himself standing on solid ground. His knees buckled as he regained his balance. A vaguely familiar door seem to generate itself from the darkness.

He reached for the handle, and before he could open the door, he was already through it. A sterile and quiet laboratory stretched out in front of him. It was his lab. The lights were dim save a few computer monitors blinking in their own proprietary rhythms. He felt a disconcerted intrigue and pushed his way further into the lab.

Papers and file folders were strewn about carelessly. This wasn't how he remembered it. As he moved deeper, he heard faint voices. They were discussing something quietly. “What can we do about him?” asked one voice sounding very concerned, “We have been wanting to test the results of a human getting caught in a rift,” responded another. There was a short pause, not one of ethical reflection, but operational feasibility. “All the big wigs will be in that molecular transmogrify seminar tomorrow afternoon...” the first voice trailed off. Another short pause, and the other voice confirmed agreement. As he moved closer to the voices, they disappeared. He passed through the area where it sounded like they were and there was no one there.

The next room contained a large glass tube in the center and a control panel off to one side. He recognized this room. This was the large animal testing chamber. Big animals like bears or even moose would be placed in the test chamber and then they could be exposed to different phenomenon or chemicals triggered by the control panel. He saw a reflection in the glass of the chamber. It was a man's reflection. He raised his hand to block out the light and get a clearer look and jumped with the realization. He was inside the test chamber. A cadre of scientists and researchers suddenly appeared around him. They were holding clip boards and discussing technical details. He recognized each of their faces. It was his team. The lead researcher glanced into the test chamber and giggled, “You guys ready to make history?” he guffawed. He was now looking at his team of researchers from inside the test chamber. Why were they doing this to him?! They didn't look on with indifference, but sadistic malice. They were enjoying it. “Rift expansion activated,” said another voice as a button clicked. The static-carbon interface jolted to life and the entire test chamber began buzzing. The chamber whirred and vibrated as the research team watched with morbid amusement. One marked notes down on a pad of paper and another wiped her eyes in disbelief. “Let's see if he makes it to the other side."

Chapter 3
Seam of Guilt

A burning electrical shock coursed through his body as a blinding white light filled his vision. For a moment, he was nowhere. There was a sharp flash and he was standing back in his lab, only this time, it was dilapidated and lay in ruin like it had been abandoned for eons. The panels on the walls were missing or falling out, the computer equipment sat cold and disengaged. There was almost a sort of organic death to the place. Guilt shot through him and then faded like a hot knife slicing through skin and cauterizing the wound. He didn't know why he felt it, he just knew that he did. As he moved down the long hallway, he noticed the lights flickering in a pattern he didn't recognize. He turned around to track his progress, and thought he saw something moving in the shadows between the flashes of light. It was probably best to keep moving forward. The flickering became more intense and eventually the light itself began melting and dripping down on the floor. Small glowing puddles of light formed on the floor as swiftly moved down the hall. He heard laughing coming from an air vent by the floor. “Hello?” he asked in curious desperation. The laughing stopped and he was left alone in silence once again.

He passed the large conference room and rounded the corner to the lab where classified experiments were performed. As he was about to pass by the lab, the double doors slid open with a pneumatic hiss, inviting him to enter. He paused for a few seconds and glanced through the doors. A dark figure stepped into his view and just stood there as though it was watching him. He could see the figure fidgeting back and forth in place. Walking towards the door, he kept his eyes on the dark apparition. It's quick, unnatural movements became more exaggerated as he closed in. When he was about ten feet in front of the figure, it bolted to its right and disappeared into the ambiance. “You lied to him about the risks,” a melancholic voice bellowed out from the shadows, catching him off-guard and causing him to stumble backwards. He recognized the voice; it belonged to one of his research assistants. “You didn't have to do that,” the voice rang out again followed by laughter, mocking him.

“He made his own decision!” He screamed back at the voice. There was no response. He felt the sharp pain return to the back of his neck. It dug into the base of his skull and angled itself downward. He couldn't move. He felt something pierce his throat from behind like he was being stabbed through the back of his neck. He screamed out in agony. His mind raced as he spun around looking for the perpetrator. He was alone. He put his hand to the back of his neck and felt nothing. No wound, no blood, no sharp object. The phantom knife sliced through his neck again and this time, cut down to the middle of his sternum before the pain disappeared completely. He fell to the ground and his breathing heavy. That was...uncomfortable. He caught his breath and returned to his feet.

The further he moved into the lab, the more dilapidated it became. Missing panels turned into bare walls with exposed electrical wires. Broken ceiling tiles became unframed roofs where the syrupy toxic daylight from outside would pour in. The text on the computer terminals was leaking off the screen and puddling in the crevices of the keyboard below. He felt that something was very wrong here. The lab was dying. He continued past the half-framed walls and mismatched furniture to the end of the hallway. He had reached a single elaborately etched wooden door with a retinal scanner on the wall to its right. There were no other avenues, this was the only way forward. Staring at it for a minute, he realized he recognized the door. It was his door, his office door.

He cautiously approached the retinal scanner and lined his eyes up with the viewport. He expected a brief pause followed by a short ding to confirm his identity and open the door. Instead, there was a loud, vomitous retching sound. He recoiled, but his vision was involuntarily glued to the retinal scanner. It wanted to show him something. He saw his face as a young man, an honest researcher who wanted to help people. The image flickered and he saw himself again, but this time much older. He was helping his staff burn reports. It flickered again and this time, he saw flashes of poison tablets. Blood splattered clothing. A pit of dead mutilated bodies. They kept flashing before him, crashing through his psyche like a wrecking ball. Eventually, they receded and he was left in darkness. Pulling his head away from the scanner, he rubbed his eyes recalling everything he just witnessed.

As he stood there in quiet contemplation, there was a familiar ding and the office door clicked open, now unlocked. Before he could reach for the door knob, the door swung open, slamming on the wall behind it. As he walked through the familiar door, he noticed that the office beyond it was anything but familiar. It was a single, dim room with a large mirror on the far wall. There was no furniture or décor. The walls were bare concrete. His foot dragged across the floor as he walked, but he wasn't sure why. He could feel the sharp pain in his neck slowly ramping up in intensity. Right now, it was just barely there, but it was noticeable. He shuffled over to the large mirror and gazed at his own reflection. It was not. Or maybe, he was not. The mirror had, not cracks, but repaired seams all over it. He didn't see his face or really anything he could recognize. He saw a dark shadow of a person. He waved his hand and the ethereal form mimicked his movements. He looked deeper into the mirror and could see a figure struggling to move in the distance.

He focused his gaze and saw that it was a man, or at least, most of a man. The skin on his face and head had been eaten away, his forearm and lower leg were missing, but he was still trudging on. Pinning his body against the wall, he was relying on sliding himself forward by synchronizing the movements of his ailing limbs. The man comes to the top of a jagged staircase. He pauses, likely trying to figure out how to surmount this new challenge, when a divine voice calls out:

Each painful step moves me closer.
Out of the shadows of dishonor.
Into the light of absolution.

The deformed figure slowly descended the wicked staircase step by step as he watched on with horrific nostalgia. “Camden, I didn't mean for it...” he trailed off. He couldn't finish the sentence. The refrain repeated itself again, louder. He tried to mouth it, but he couldn't. He tried to methodically say each word and it wouldn't come out. “Each painful...step...” he stuttered, “keeps them compliant. Through shadows and dishonor,” the words came out of his mouth, but they were not his own, “we spoil the road to absolution,” he finished.

He was unable to repeat the refrain, but something compelled him to. The sharp pain in the back of his neck pushed deeply into his throat before shooting up through his brain. His teeth ached and his gums bled. He collapsed on the ground as the mirror faded to black and the glass shattered with force, spreading shards of itself across the empty room.

Chapter 4
Silence of Neglect and Drain of Corruption

Picking glass shards from his sullen skin, he slowly rises to his feet. The mirror lay in a million pieces before him, all of them contaminated with the poison of his past decisions. The section of the wall that the mirror previously occupied now led into a dark cavernous expanse. He passed through the threshold and felt the pain in his neck ratchet up a few levels. The darkness eventually gave way to an orphanage. The pastel décor and glossy paint of the walls contrasted with the heavy air and dim lighting. Children's drawings adorned the walls along with signs about hand washing and general courtesy. He was standing in a hallway with several doors on either side. Each door was a different color and had a sign with a name on it. The air smelled of mildew and old paper.

He passed doorway after doorway, the names on the signs never repeating as the hallway seemed to extend into oblivion. He kept going. The scent of mildew hung heavy in the air as he dragged himself down the hallway. The light dimmed and he noticed all of the doors started to become the same color: a light auburn. He slowed down to get a better look at the signs. They all read "Margaret." One of the doors, exactly the same as the others, felt like it had grabbed him and held him in place. The only thing he could do was walk towards it, moving in any other direction wasn't possible. His arms and legs felt locked in position. He slowly inched closer to the door, the name "Margaret" getting larger by the moment. Something compelled him to open it. He reached forward and his hand seized the door knob, clutching it tightly. He turned the knob, but the door wouldn't open. It was locked from the other side. "Dad?" a small voice broke through the close door, "Did you come back for me?" it asked, dejected but hopeful. He tried to speak, but his mouth refused his commands and his voice wasn't present.

He reached for the door knob again, this time it melted in his hand. A viscous black sludge dripped through his fingers. The voice became more anxious, "Please, dad. Get me out of here!" it pleaded. He banged his hands against the door, but it didn't budge. He heard the knob jiggle on the other side like whoever was on the other side was turning it, but it still wouldn't open. The door is locked, he wanted to yell, but was unable to. His voice box seized and he couldn't get the words out. The knob kept turning in a futile attempt at escape. "Why did you forget about me, dad?!" the voice was hysterical now. He stepped back, unable to do anything. The screaming continued for what felt like an eternity as he impotently witnessed it. "This wasn't my intention..." he was finally able to blurt out, "I didn't want that to...happen to him," he protested. There was a long pause and the voice replied, "you knew exactly what would happen to him."

He started crying, but there were no tears, just a stream of smoldering ashes pouring down his face. “I didn't mean it, I swear!” The voice was silent. He banged on the door again, still nothing. He was about to turn and leave when the door gently whined open. He ran through the decrepit doorway expecting to enter a child's room, but this was anything but. The pastel colors had been replaced with a clinical white paint and the children's drawings had become safety protocols. He was back in his lab. As he turned back, he was looking through a large window at a man sitting at a table. He had his head in his hands and appeared to be sobbing heavily. He was holding a picture of a little girl. He wasn't saying anything, just crying uncontrollably. The door opened and another man walked in...it was himself. He sat down at the table and said something to the man. He couldn't hear what was being said, but he could tell by their body language that it was important. The man looked up and he instantly recognized him. It was Jonathan Camden.

He watched himself on the other side of the glass slide a packet of papers with a pen on top over to Camden. He stared at the papers for a moment and asked a question. His hopes seemed to be quickly dashed and he began flipping through the papers in front of him. The scratching of the pen was deafening. Signing each form in triplicate, he reluctantly slid the packet back across the table and resigned himself to staring blankly while quietly sobbing. The papers were reviewed and he watched himself leave the room without saying a word to Camden. The scene froze like a video feed interrupted and he was left standing there staring at a broken man.

The window flashed a sticky black that seemed to ooze from the glass before settling on an image of a man laying on an examination table, motionless with dark sutures and clear tubing with black liquid running through it attached to various parts of his body. He turned around and he was in the operating room. When he glanced back at the man on the table, he was less than five feet away from him. He saw folders on the nearby table that had the numbers “0598” scrawled across them in a hurry. He glanced back at the man, and realized that it was Jonathan Camden. He saw himself again, this time much older and grayer. He casually walked up to Camden, this time with an air of authority, and touched some device attached to the man's head. “The neural interface is online and working exceptionally well,” he said as the other researchers nodded in agreement and marked notes down in their journals.

He looked very pleased with himself, and he was, at least as far as he could remember. Another researcher approached him with a vexed look on their face. The researcher tapped him on the shoulder and shoved a clipboard in his face, “The subject is experiencing very high levels of cortisol. His physiological response is borderline. We need to stop this,” the man said, dripping with concern, not for Camden, but for the integrity of the experiment. “No,” he said sharply causing the researcher to lower the clipboard. “I am not going to lose another test subject just because someone someone feels 'icky,'” he said, scrunching up his face and making a quotation gesture with his fingers. “This time it will be a success.”

As he said that, Camden's eyes bolted open. His gaze was fixed straight ahead on the ceiling above. “Fantastic,” he heard himself say. Even the concerned researcher was marveling at what was happening. There was a loud groan and the reanimated cadaver lunged to a sitting position. The entire research team gasped in unison. The corpse of Camden lumbered to its feet and stared straight ahead at him through the window. “Can you see me?” he said loudly while staring back. Camden's eyes were dead and unfeeling. He didn't acknowledge him. He just eyed him unflinchingly. There was a sharp tearing pain in the back of his neck that cut up through his head and exited from his temples. He screamed in pain and grabbed his head. When he stood up again, he was in absolute darkness and Camden's visage was burned into his mind, watching him, waiting for him. He was there every time he closed his eyes. The ground shook and a doorway of bone and viscera formed in front of him. The sharp pain returned and the back of his neck was on fire. He saw a brief flash of himself in the door, but it was a mangled mess and slightly off like the townspeople. Fear and guilt shot through him, chasing each other through his nervous system on an endless loop. He pushed the rigid door open and he could see the town of Greyrow through the doorway. The darkness of the room gave way to a border of light around it. Then he heard the voice from before bellow out:

Each painful step moves me closer.
Out of the shadows of dishonor.
Into the light of absolution.

The words still failed to form in his mouth. He could barely remember the syllables.

Chapter 5
The Threading of Grace

He lifted his leg to step through the doorway and he could feel it pushing him through like a guest who has overstayed their welcome. He once again, felt the abrasive sandy ground of Greyrow scraping the bottom of his feet. The town looked familiar, but different. Some of the buildings had outgrowths at impossible angles. They were shapes with an every shifting amount of sides. At first, it appeared that the Post Office had only four walls. Upon closer inspection, it had seven. Turning the corner, revealed nine, and coming around full circle showed only three. Shadows appeared at the wrong angle, and water flowed backwards. He could see the townspeople in the distance. They were standing completely still. Not moving. Not talking. Not breathing.

His leg began dragging again and he felt a sharp pain in his right forearm. The townspeople watched him move closer, regarding him with contempt. All eyes followed his limping progression across the town square. He was careful to avoid making physical contact with them. Once he was deep into the town square and surrounded by a large crowd of bystanders, he stopped to catch his breath. His dragging foot was affecting his stamina. His chest heaving, there was a collective groan from the crowd around him and they began coming to life and closing in on him. Feeling strangely panicked, he started moving away from the town center. They eventually surrounded him and forced him down a side alleyway.

He was forced into a courtyard, and fell onto his knees as the crowd advanced. One by one, they came over to him and spoke in voices that weren't their own. An elderly woman with her nose bent at a right angle and an eye in the center of her forehead was first. Her gaze was empty as she opened her mouth, almost unhinging it. “She died because you said nothing!” scolded a young woman's voice as the elderly woman's mouth hung agape. She repeated this incessantly as the pitch of her voice became higher and higher until it was just a constant squeal. Her head recoiled back, bouncing around on her neck as though it hadn't been properly attached. Her gaze, still fixed on him.

A young man walked up to him and grabbed his shoulder. His face was flush with anger, “You condemned them. All of them. You did this!” the man poked his finger firmly into his chest. He tried pushing him back, but the man overpowered him. “I didn't mean...it was an accident. You have to believe me!” he cried. Every justification was met with indifference. A ragged man stopped him, pressing his palm into his chest. He looked him deep in the eyes and the man said “Why did you do this to my father?” in a young woman's voice as his mouth moved out of sync with his words. His mind flashed back to the image of the auburn door and signed papers. “Margaret...I'm...sorry,” he wept, as he was swept up by the crowd, unable to do anything.

The crowd pushed him further into the town until he was in a tight courtyard with a strange device in the center. It was a tall black structure covered in pitted metal with several lines of sinew intersecting its core. It was calling to him. He could feel a deep pulsing panic wash over him. He stepped forward. He inched towards the machine unwittingly but automatically. The townspeople were now gathered around him, watching with an eerie exuberance. The ground shook and the crowd began chanting:

Flesh to thread, seal the shame.
Thread the wound, bind his pain.
Let his sins remember him.

It repeated over and over in a sickly uneven manner. The unbalanced meter of the chant was disorienting and left him reeling. The chanting continued as the ground rumbled again, this time right underneath him. He could feel the machinations of something big springing to life. The sky split open and a torrent of hellfire raced across it like flame to dry newspaper. The chanting got louder as the mob closed in around him, forcing his back against the black pitted metal frame of the unholy device.

His eyes darted from side to side, from face to grotesque face. They wanted something from him, and they were going to take it. A voice pierced through his consciousness, reciting a familiar verse:

Each painful step moves me closer.
Out of the shadows of dishonor.
Into the light of absolution.

It echoed in his head like ringing bell. He attempted to say the words, and they were birthed out of order and disfigured. He tried again, to no avail. The words just kept repeating in his head. They drown out the chanting of the townspeople. He gathered his strength and deliberately willed each word into existence, “Each painful step, moves me...” he stumbled for a moment, but regained his footing, “closer. Out of the shadows of dishonor. Into the light...” a cutting pain sliced across his abdomen in perpendicular directions, forcing him to the ground, “...of absolution,” he choked out, pulling himself up to a sitting position.

The ground trembled harder than before and the townspeople started cheering. It wasn't a joyous cheer, but a jeering mocking wail. The massive machinery behind him awoke and the entire hulking metal apparatus wrenched backwards violently. A tiny spike appeared on the tip. The crowd was wide-eyed and silent, intently watching what was unfolding in front of them. He waited patiently as a cool calm overtook his body. His work was done. There was another guttural howl from somewhere nearby and the metal arm of the machine shot forward faster than it had pulled back, penetrating the back of his neck, right at the base of his skull. It lifted him high into the air and held him there. His mind was clear and he was at peace. Whatever this was, it was necessary.

With a black spike protruding through his head, he gently swayed in the humid breeze. The sinew lines connected to the black metal detached on one end and freely hung from its hulking base. The loose tendrils whipped into the air as the ends each formed into a sharp metal point. They first pierced his legs, then his arms, and finally his head. Once they passed through one direction, they circled back and went through the other way stitching up his entire body. Once the stitching was done, they were pulled tight and set. After a few seconds, he began screaming from inside his sinew prison, but his muffled screams fell on deaf ears. The sinew drew tight and then lax. With a hushed pop each tie began to sever and his body was ripped in half and reassembled inside-out. His internal organs still gurgling and pulsing. The crowd continued to watch, silently and enthralled.

With a heavy shudder, his cocoon undulated hard like something was building up inside it. Finally, it burst apart, chunks of bone, viscera, and sinew plopping onto the ground. A grotesque form now shown upon the crowd. Burnt and mangled body parts connected by rotten veins and diseased tendons now lay before them. A living organism broken down and remade into a horrifying mockery of life. He spent his life taking advantage of others for personal gain, and this is what he has to show for it. Rather, what he is to show others. A deep tranquility overcame him. This was just. It was right. They didn't make him a monster, he did that.

They just remembered him.

www.ingramcontent.com/pod-product-compliance
Lightning Source LLC
LaVergne TN
LVHW090616110826
845146LV00001B/418